TYLER FREE LIBRARY
81A MOOSUP VALLEY RD.
FOSTER, RI 02825

 WONDER BOOKS

Cats

The Sound of Short A

By Alice K. Flanagan

The Child's World®, Inc.

See the cat in the hat.

See the cat on the mat.

See the cat in a lap.

See the cat have a nap.

See the cat in a jam.

See the cat play
with Pam.

See the cat on her back.

See the cat play
with Jack.

See the cat give a tug.

See the cat hide under the rug.

Word List

back	jam
cat	lap
hat	mat
have	nap
Jack	Pam

Note to Parents and Educators

The books in the Phonics series of the Wonder Books are based on current research which supports the idea that our brains are pattern detectors rather than rules appliers. This means children learn to read easier when they are taught the familiar spelling patterns found in English. As children encounter more complex words, they have greater success in figuring out these words by using the spelling patterns.

Throughout the 35 books, the texts provide the reader with the opportunity to practice and apply knowledge of the sounds in natural language. The 10 books on the long and short vowels introduce the sounds using familiar onsets and rimes, or spelling patterns, for reinforcement. For example, the word "cat" might be used to present the short "a" sound, with the letter "c" being the onset and "-at" being the rime. This approach provides practice and reinforcement of the short "a" sound, as there are many familiar words made with the "-at" rime.

The 21 consonants and the 4 blends ("ch," "sh," "th," and "wh") use many of these same rimes. The letter(s) before the vowel in a word are considered the onset. Changing the onset allows the series to maintain the practice and reinforcement of the rimes. The repeated use of a word or phrase reinforces the target sound.

The number on the spine of each book facilitates arranging the books in the order that children acquire each sound. The books can also be arranged into groups of long vowels, short vowels, consonants, and blends. All the books in each grouping have their numbers printed in the same color on the spine. The books can be grouped and regrouped easily and quickly, depending on the teacher's needs.

The stories and accompanying photographs in this series are based on time-honored concepts in children's literature: Well-written, engaging texts and colorful, high-quality photographs combine to produce books that children want to read again and again.

Dr. Peg Ballard
Minnesota State University, Mankato

Photo Credits

All photos © copyright: Dembinsky Photo Associates: 4 (Larime Photographic); Photri: 3 (H. G. Ross); Tony Stone Images: 7, 11 (George Haling), 8 (Rolf Kopfle), 12 (Tom Dietrich), 15, 19 (Kathi Lamm), 16, 20 (Timothy Shonnard). Cover: Tony Stone Images/Bruno Dittrich.

Photo Research: Alice Flanagan
Design and production: Herman Adler Design Group

Text copyright © 2000 by The Child's World®, Inc.

All rights reserved. No part of this book may be reproduced or utilized in any form or by any means without written permission from the publisher.
Printed in the United States of America.

Library of Congress Cataloging-in-Publication Data

Flanagan, Alice K.
    Cats : the sound of "short a" / by Alice K. Flanagan.
        p. cm. — (Wonder books)
    Summary : Simple text and repetition of the letter "a" help readers learn how to use this sound.
    ISBN 1-56766-691-4 (library reinforced : alk. paper)
    [1. Cats Fiction. 2. Alphabet. 3. Stories in rhyme.] I. Title. II. Series: Wonder books (Chanhassen, Minn.)
PZ8.3.F6365Cat   1999
[E]—dc21   99-25500
                                                        CIP

3 6009 00019 8365

MAY 0 0

TYLER FREE LIBRARY

2 6009 00019 8300

DATE DUE

	OCT 1 6 2004	
SEP 6 '00		
OCT 1 8 '00		
JUL 1 3 01	FEB 2 4 2006	
SEP 1 0 01		
	AUG 2 0 2005	
DEC 1 2 '01		
SEP 0 6 '02	JUN 2 1 2006	
NOV 27 02	APR 1 3 2007	
MAR 0 1 '03		
	JUL 1 1 2008	
MAY 1 2 03		
NOV 2 6 2003	AUG 0 1 2008	
	AUG 2 6 2008	
DEC 1 9 2003		
MAR 1 7 2004		
SEP 2 0 2004		

Demco, Inc. 38-293